Licensed exclusively to Top That Publishing Ltd
Tide Mill Way, Woodbridge, Suffolk, IP12 1AP, UK
www.topthatpublishing.com
Copyright © 2014 Tide Mill Media
All rights reserved
0 2 4 6 8 9 7 5 3 1
Printed and bound in China

ISBN 978-1-78244-786-3

A catalogue record for this book is available from the British Library

Giggle!
Giggle!

Growl, roar, growl, growl, roar,
Tiger has the world's most tickly paws!
He's the most ticklish tiger you'll ever see,
Swimming in pools and climbing trees.

Giggle!
Giggle!

Growl, roar, growl, growl, roar,
Tiger has a tickly chin and a tickly jaw!
When he steps on a termite mound,
He makes a funny giggling sound.

Giggle! Giggle!

Growl, roar, growl, growl, roar,
Tiger has a tickly tail and much, much more!
When Monkey tweaks his tail in play,
Tiger laughs and laughs all day!

Giggle! Giggle!

Growl, roar, growl, growl, roar,
Tiger can't face being tickled any more!
This ticklish tiger is homeward bound,
But he'll always make his giggling sound.

Giggle! Giggle!

Stomp, rumble, stomp, rumble,
Elephants are hiding in the jungle!
Papa Elephant is the biggest of all!
He makes the loudest trumpeting call!

Trumpet! Trumpet!

Stomp, rumble, stomp, rumble,
Elephants are hiding in the jungle!
Mama Elephant has on her favourite scarf.
The sight makes Little Bird laugh and laugh!

Trumpet! Trumpet!

Stomp, rumble, stomp, rumble,
Elephants are hiding in the jungle!
Brother Elephant plays with his ball,
So busy he doesn't hear Papa's loud call.

Trumpet! Trumpet!

Stomp, rumble, stomp, rumble,
Elephants are hiding in the jungle!
Sister Elephant is young and still quite short,
She giggles and makes a cute-sounding snort!

Trumpet!
Trumpet!

Stomp, rumble, stomp, rumble,
Elephants are hiding in the jungle!
Here's the Elephant Family, together at last,
Trumpeting, stomping and rumbling past!

Trumpet! Trumpet!